AKIMBO
AND THE
BABOONS

ALEXANDER McCALL SMITH

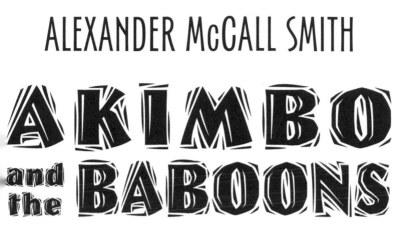

AKIMBO
and the BABOONS

ILLUSTRATED BY LeUyen Pham

BLOOMSBURY
CHILDREN'S
BOOKS

Published by Bloomsbury U.S.A. Children's Books
175 Fifth Avenue, New York, New York 10010

Library of Congress Cataloging-in-Publication Data
McCall Smith, Alexander.
Akimbo and the baboons / by Alexander McCall Smith ;
illustrated by LeUyen Pham.—1st U.S. ed.
p.   cm.
Summary: Akimbo and his cousin Kosi accompany a scientist into
the African bush to study the behavior of a troop of baboons.
ISBN-13: 978-1-59990-215-9 • ISBN-10: 1-59990-215-X (hardcover)
[1. Baboons—Fiction. 2. Africa—Fiction.] I. Pham, LeUyen, ill.
II. Title.
PZ7.M47833755Ah2008   [Fic]—dc22   2008017212

First U.S. Edition 2008
Typeset by Westchester Book Composition
Printed in the U.S.A. by Worzalla
2   4   6   8   10   9   7   5   3   1

The author's royalties from this book are being donated to
The Lady Khama Trust in Botswana for charitable purposes
connected with the welfare of children.

All papers used by Bloomsbury U.S.A. are natural,
recyclable products made from wood grown in well-managed
forests. The manufacturing processes conform to the
environmental regulations of the country of origin.

CONTENTS

Special Visitors   1

Into the Bush   9

A Close Call   17

Lunchtime Lesson   24

Tommy and Ben   32

Baboon Rescue   40

Off Track   49

Help!   57

Did You Know?   65

SPECIAL VISITORS

There are some days that just feel exciting, right from the beginning, and this was one of them.

School had finished for the year, and a whole month of doing exactly as he pleased stretched out in front of Akimbo. That was thrilling enough, but to make things better, this was the day that his cousin, Kosi, was due to arrive for a three-week stay. He was the same age as Akimbo, or almost—Akimbo had been born two days before he was, and that made a big difference, or so Akimbo sometimes said.

Kosi liked coming to stay with Akimbo. Not only were the two boys good friends,

1

but for Kosi, who lived in a town, it was a chance to stay on the great game reserve where Akimbo's father was the head ranger. This was a real treat for him, and he always counted the days until his uncle, Akimbo's father, picked him up at the station in his truck.

So there was a lot of excitement that morning when Kosi arrived and carried his things into the room he was to share with Akimbo. But there was more to come.

"We're having another visitor today," announced Akimbo's father. "The baboon lady is arriving at lunchtime."

Akimbo looked at his father. "The baboon lady?" he asked. He had not heard of anybody called that before and he wondered what it meant. Was this a lady baboon? Or was it a woman who had a pet baboon?

His father saw Akimbo's confusion and smiled. "No," he said, "she's not a baboon. She's a scientist. She's one of these people who studies baboons. And she knows a lot about them, I can tell you!"

Akimbo was a little disappointed. He liked baboons, which he thought were even cleverer than monkeys, and it would have been interesting to have a visiting baboon. He and Kosi could have played with her, he imagined, and if the baboon behaved well enough, she might have been allowed to sit at the table while they had their meals. Now all he had to look forward to was a scientist.

"You'll like her," his father went on. "She's lived with baboons, you know. They treated her like another baboon."

Kosi laughed. "And did she eat what they ate?" he inquired.

"You can ask her yourself," said Akimbo's father. "Ask her about it at lunch."

The two boys had plenty to occupy themselves with that morning, and lunchtime seemed to come around very quickly. They had seen no sign of the baboon lady, but when Akimbo's mother sent a message over to the ranger office that lunch was ready, the boys saw Akimbo's father walking to the house with a tall woman carrying a satchel over her shoulder.

"My name is Jenny," said the woman as she shook the boys' hands. "But some people

just call me Jen. So you can do that if you want to."

Akimbo liked Jen immediately. She had a warm smile that seemed to hover around her lips all the time, as if somebody had just said something funny, or was about to. And Akimbo could tell that Kosi liked her too.

He wondered what she was doing in the game reserve. Animal scientists often came to see his father, and they usually had some project or other that they wanted to do. Sometimes they just wanted to count a particular kind of animal. Sometimes they wanted to tag the animals to learn where they migrated. And sometimes they wanted to take blood samples, to send off to their laboratories for testing. That was easy enough with some animals, but with others it involved putting the animal to sleep for a while with a special dart. That could be dangerous— not only for the animal, but also for the people who had to get close enough to fire the dart.

It soon became clear at lunchtime what Jen planned to do.

"Perhaps you could tell the boys what your plans are," said Akimbo's father. "I know that they're interested."

"You're interested in baboons?" asked Jen. "Well, I'm not surprised, boys. They are fascinating creatures. They're a lot like us, you know—like you and me."

She began to explain what she was planning to do. With the agreement of Akimbo's father, his men had built a small hut in a part of the reserve where there was a large pack of baboons. Over the next two weeks, Jen was going to live out there, night and day, and while she was doing this, she was going to watch the habits of the baboons.

"There's something I particularly want to find out," Jen said. "I want to see how they share their food."

Akimbo looked surprised. He did not think that animals shared their food very much. He thought it was first come, first served—most of the time.

"Do they really share?" he asked.

"Yes, they do," said Jen. "Not always, but

a lot of the time. And that's something I've been studying."

"Why?" asked Kosi, who had been silent until now.

Akimbo thought that was a silly question, but Jen took it seriously.

"I want to find out," she said, "because it helps us to understand how baboons see the world."

The two boys thought about this for a moment. Then Jen suddenly turned to Akimbo's mother and father.

"Would you let the boys come out to see what I do?" she asked. "I'm sure that they'd enjoy it."

Akimbo's father looked at his wife, who hesitated for a moment before she nodded. "If they promise to behave themselves . . . ," she began.

"They can be looked after by the junior ranger you were going to lend me as my assistant," said Jen. "I'm sure he'll watch the boys."

Akimbo's father stared down at his plate.

He looked embarrassed by something. "Actually," he began, "there's a problem there. We're very shorthanded at the ranger station, I'm afraid. Two of the men are off sick and so . . . well, we won't be able to lend you an assistant after all."

For a few moments nobody said anything. Then, quite unexpectedly, Akimbo broke the silence. "We'll help," he blurted out. "Kosi and I can be your assistants, Jen. Please!"

Again there was silence. Now it was Akimbo's father's turn to speak. "Well . . . ," he began.

It seemed to Akimbo that his father was about to say no. But Jen did not understand it this way. "Oh, thank you," she said enthusiastically. "They'll be very helpful, and I'm sure that they'll be very careful. Won't you, boys?"

Akimbo and Kosi both nodded eagerly. It was settled!

INTO THE BUSH

There was a lot to do that day if they were to be ready to leave the next morning. Jen had all the supplies that she would need for her time in the bush, but now that Akimbo and Kosi were going to join her, more provisions were needed. Fortunately, Akimbo's mother's storeroom was full, and she was able to come up with all the food and other things they would need.

"I've never been camping," Kosi said to Akimbo. "I can't wait to try it!"

Akimbo shared his cousin's enthusiasm. Of course he had spent a lot of time in the bush with his father, but this was different.

There would be no parents on this trip, and that made him feel very grown-up.

And there was another thing that made this trip special. Since they would be helping her, Jen had announced that she would pay the boys a small amount of money each day. This made Akimbo feel important. He had always helped in the past without being paid, but this would be a real job.

The next morning, when the time came to leave, the two boys helped Jen load everything into her truck and secure it for the bumpy ride ahead. They would be traveling along rough roads and they would have to make sure that nothing was damaged on the journey. Jen had some delicate equipment with her, including a telescope to watch the baboons with and a large, expensive camera. It was very important that all this was safe.

It took them five hours to reach the place where the hut had been built. They traveled through thick bush made up of tall grass and high trees, and at several points along the journey Jen had to stop to check their position. Then suddenly Akimbo saw the hut, which had been erected not far from the base of a granite hill.

"There!" he shouted. "That's the place."

Jen turned the truck off the road and they made the last of the bumpy journey through the waist-high grass. It was like driving across the sea, thought Akimbo, as he watched the grass part in front of the truck.

They came to a halt beside the hut. It was not much of a building—and you could easily miss it if you weren't looking for it. It had been made out of tree branches and the trunks of saplings, all tied together with twine and then poked firmly into the ground. There was a simple door, made out of a sheet of thin wood, and a roof of bundles of thatch.

"Well," said Jen, surveying their new home. "At least we don't have to be here for long!"

For Akimbo and Kosi, the hut was just right. Although it was dark inside—there were no windows to let in the light—it seemed comfortable enough. The floor was earth, pounded down to make it hard, and right in the middle a few stones had been stacked together to make a fireplace.

"It's perfect," said Akimbo, laying his sleeping bag down on the floor. "Can we make a fire?"

Jen suggested that they wait until evening for that, but in preparation she sent the boys out to collect firewood. Then they busied themselves with unpacking the rest of the equipment and setting up camp. At last, by midafternoon everything was in place.

"Now what?" asked Akimbo. "Do we go and find the baboons now?"

Jen shook her head. "I think that the baboons are more likely to find us," she said. "They live close by and they're very inquisitive creatures. So we'll just sit here and wait."

"Won't they be frightened of us?" asked Kosi.

Jen explained that this was unlikely. "These baboons have hardly ever seen human beings," she said. "They'll be careful, but they won't really be frightened of us. Animals that have never been harmed by human beings are often fearless."

They waited for what seemed like a very long time. Akimbo found himself itching to get up and do something, but Jen had told them that they should all just stay quiet until something happened.

And then it did. The first sign was a barking sound from the direction of the hill. Akimbo thought it was a wild dog, but then Jen raised a finger, pointed into the long grass, and smiled expectantly. So it must be a baboon.

A few minutes later, while Akimbo was looking in the opposite direction, there was a sudden movement at the edge of the clearing. Then, a few moments later, a dark shape emerged. It was the first of the baboons.

When the baboon saw Akimbo and the others sitting under the tree beside the hut, he stopped where he was. Raising himself up on his hind legs, he stared at the three strangers. Then he dropped back to his haunches and bared his teeth. They were large, discolored teeth, like fangs, and Akimbo decided he never wanted to be bitten by a baboon.

"Just stay still," whispered Jen. "Let him get used to us."

The baboon stared at them for a few

moments and then disappeared back into the grass.

"He's gone," said Kosi, sounding disappointed.

"Not for long," whispered Jen. "You'll see."

She was right. A few minutes later, the large baboon reappeared. This time he was accompanied by several other members of the troop, including a female with a tiny baby baboon holding on to her. The baby was upside down but seemed quite happy with the ride.

The baboons sat down and stared back at the people. They were making low noises, little coughs and grunts, as if they were talking to one another. Akimbo wondered what they could be saying, and if it was a special baboon language they were using. Or was it just noises?

While he was thinking this, Jen suddenly stood up. When the baboons saw her do this, they gave a start but quickly settled down.

"You boys stand up too," she said. "Don't make any other movements. Just stand up."

The two boys did as they were told, all

while the baboons watched with a mixture of wariness and curiosity. Then, after a couple of minutes, the first baboon gave a grunt, and the whole group turned around and loped off into the grass again.

Jen looked at the boys, rubbing her hands together with satisfaction. She seemed pleased.

"Good!" she said. "They've taken a good look at us, and they know about us. So tomorrow we can approach them, and they won't be too worried."

The boys had hoped to see more of the baboons, but at least this was a start. And there were things to do now—they had to make the fire, since it would soon become dark, and they would need to cook dinner. So everybody was busy and had no time to think of the night ahead and what it might bring.

A CLOSE CALL

fter they finished their meal, Jen and the boys sat outside the entrance to the hut, listening to the sounds of the African night. In the background there was the chirrup of insects, a shrill sound that became louder and then softer in waves. Then, from time to time, there were other sounds—the shriek of a nocturnal bird of prey, the grunt of some creature scurrying its way through the undergrowth. The night was not quiet.

Nor was it dark. No sooner had the sun gone down than an almost full moon floated up over the hills. It bathed the bush in a soft light that seemed to make the whole world a place of mysterious shapes and shadows. Was that a bush or an elephant? Of course it was just a bush, but hadn't it moved? "It was just the wind," said Jen. Just the wind.

After a while it was time to go to bed. They had all brought sleeping bags and had made beds for themselves out of grass and leaves. Akimbo put a couple of large logs on the fire they had made in the center of the hut, and this comforted them as they snuggled down into their sleeping bags.

"I hope there are no lions near here," said Kosi in a small voice. This was all very different from his room back in the town where he lived.

"There are," said Akimbo. "But the fire will keep them away. Don't worry."

Kosi felt very frightened. He was glad, though, that he had his older cousin with him—and this really was one of those times when it mattered that Akimbo was two days older.

It was Akimbo who woke up first in the middle of the night. He wasn't sure what had awoken him, but it was a noise of some kind. He wondered whether it was a lion, and he was relieved to see that the fire in the hut was still glowing strongly. He listened carefully.

He heard the noise again. This time it was louder, and he knew exactly what it was. It was a baboon barking. And now there was more barking, louder and angrier than before. This time it woke up Jen, and then Kosi.

"What's going on?" Akimbo whispered.

"Something's happening at their sleeping place," said Jen, rubbing the sleep out of her eyes.

"Can we go and see?" asked Akimbo.

Jen looked doubtful. You did not walk around the African bush at night unless you had a very good reason to do so. But now the baboons had started to howl, and Jen got out of her sleeping bag.

"We can go and take a look," she said. "We'll take the flashlights."

The boys slipped out of their sleeping bags and put on their shoes. As usual, Akimbo held his shoes upside down for a few seconds, just in case a scorpion had decided to make its bed in one of them. Then, walking in single file behind Jen, they began to make their way through the bush toward the sound of the distressed baboons.

The baboons slept between rocks at the foot of the nearby granite hill. Jen explained that this was a good place for them since they could tuck themselves away in little spaces and caves between the boulders, and this kept them warm and safe during the night. As they approached the rocks, Jen told the boys to turn off their flashlights so they could observe what was happening without frightening the baboons even more.

At first, even in the moonlight, it was hard to make out which shadows were baboons and which were rocks. But then, as they crouched not far away and stared at the scene, they were able to make out the shapes of the baboons and watch their movements.

A number of the baboons had climbed up onto the top of the boulders and were swaying around, howling and barking in alarm. Others were still in their little caves and were barking out from there, their voices echoing against the walls of rock.

"Something's really upsetting them," whispered Jen. "Something that—"

She did not finish. At that moment, Akimbo gave a cry and reached out to pull Jen to the ground just as the large shape of an animal hurled itself across the place where she had been crouching only seconds before. At the same time he pulled her down, he switched on his flashlight.

The shape shot past, but it was still caught for an instant in the beam of Akimbo's flashlight. And it was long enough for all of them to realize that what had leaped past them was a leopard—a leopard that had now vanished into the darkness behind them.

For a moment nobody was able to speak. Then Jen brushed herself off and switched on her own flashlight. In the background, not far away, a few of the braver baboons had ventured out and were staring at the three unexpected visitors. A large baboon took a few steps forward, sniffed at the air, and then

grunted. This seemed to calm the rest of the troop, who now stopped barking and howling.

"So that's what was going on," said Jen. "A leopard. Their most deadly enemy."

She turned to Akimbo and shook his hand. "You saved me there," she said. "That leopard would have mauled me badly if you hadn't pulled me to the ground."

Akimbo didn't know what to say—he did not think of himself as a hero. It had all happened so quickly that he had not even thought about it. He had seen the sudden movement and realized that Jen was in danger; his reactions had done the rest.

They made their way back to the hut in silence. Akimbo was relieved that everything had worked out well. They had saved the baboons from their enemy, and at the same time Jen had not been hurt. It could have turned out very differently, of course, but he did not think about that. And soon they were back in the hut, safely back in their sleeping bags, with their fire burning bright, keeping them safe through the African night, safe until morning.

Lunchtime Lesson

The baboons will be very upset," said Jen the next morning. "Most of the time they can look after themselves, but leopards can still take them. They go for the baboons on the edge of the troop and it's over pretty quickly, I'm afraid."

Akimbo nodded. Having been brought up on the game reserve, he knew that these things happened in nature, but he still found it sad to think about.

They were walking very quietly to a place near the hill where they would spend the day watching the baboons. Jen had explained that after the night's disturbances, the baboons would probably stay close to home. It would be a day or two, she thought, before they started foraging for food again.

She was right. When they reached their destination, they could see the large baboons sitting on rocks while down below them the youngsters played some game of their own.

"They love playing," said Jen as she set up her telescope under the shade of a tree. "Look at those two over there."

Akimbo and Kosi looked in the direction she was pointing. Two small baboons, not much bigger than an ordinary cat, were pushing each other over in the dust. One seized the other's tail and gave it a sharp tug, while the other spun around and tried to fend off his attacker with blows and nips. Then they tumbled around together until another young baboon strolled across and distracted them.

"They have long friendships," Jen explained as she peered through the lens of her telescope. "And they live in families."

"Just like us?" asked Akimbo.

"Yes," said Jen. "Just like us. But a little different. You see that group over there, where the little ones are playing? I'm pretty sure that's a family. But it's mostly females and children; the males are sitting together over there. Do you see them?"

She beckoned the boys over to the telescope and invited them to look through it. Akimbo went first. He saw a group of large baboons sitting near a flat rock. They were peering out over the top of the grass, as if keeping guard.

"They're on sentry duty," Jen explained. "They'll be looking out for that leopard, or for any other threat, for that matter. They've seen us, but I think they know that we're all right."

"Will they remember that we scared the leopard off?" asked Kosi.

"They might," said Jen. "They're very intelligent creatures, after all. But it's always difficult to tell what an animal is thinking. We can't assume that they think the same way as we do."

"But you said they had friends," Akimbo pointed out.

"Yes," Jen said. "They do. So I suppose

they feel fondness for others. Look over there. That's how they show it."

She pointed to a small group of baboons that were sitting near the playing youngsters. It was Kosi's turn with the telescope now, and as he focused it on the baboons he let out a gasp. "She's combing her friend's hair!" he said. "Look! She's using her fingers as a comb."

"That's called grooming," said Jen. "They'll do that for hours and hours. They love it. And it's how baboons make friends for life."

For the next few hours, the boys sat with Jen under the tree while she made notes in her notebook. They did not have much to do, but every so often she asked them to count the number of baboons in a group while she wrote the results down. It was not very exciting for Akimbo and Kosi, but Jen explained that there was always a lot of watching in science first and the fun would come later. "The fun always comes," she said. "Believe me."

And it did. Some hours later, just when Akimbo thought that the baboons would do nothing that day, two of them suddenly detached themselves from the others and started to edge their way toward the small group of people under the tree.

"Don't frighten them," whispered Jen. "Just let them come."

The baboons inched forward and then stopped and sat down. Silently they stared at the people, looking at them as if they were trying to make out what on earth these strange creatures could be doing under the tree. Then they took a few steps closer, very casually, as if they wanted to give the impression that they were just going for an afternoon walk. Having come a little closer, they sat down and stared again.

After a while, the two visiting baboons were close enough for Akimbo and Kosi to study their expressions easily. This made the baboons open their eyes wide at them, as if they were making faces. Jen smiled at this.

"They're trying to tell you something," she whispered to the boys. "They're trying to tell you that this is their place and you should have asked first before you came here. That's what all that means."

Then it happened, and it happened so quickly that neither Akimbo nor Kosi had the time to stop it. They had been eating their lunch, which consisted of two sandwiches Jen had made for them. When the two baboons had started to approach, the boys put their sandwiches down on the grass so they could finish them later. Or that's what they thought; the baboons had something quite different in mind.

With a sudden whooping sound, the baboons dashed forward and snatched the sandwiches. Then, as quickly as they had darted in, they scampered off to a safe distance. They sat down, and watching the boys carefully, they stuffed the half-eaten sandwiches into their mouths.

"Our lunch!" wailed Akimbo indignantly.

Jen laughed. "Sorry about that," she said. "It's a lesson that I also had to learn when I first got to know these animals. They love to steal."

"But it's not fair," said Kosi crossly. He was hungry and the only food was back at the hut.

"The baboons think it's perfectly fair," said Jen. "They were hungry; they saw some sandwiches. It was as simple as that."

Akimbo and Kosi looked at each other. Jen was right, and they both decided that the best thing to do was to laugh. After all, it had been pretty funny, and the baboons looked very pleased with themselves.

"All right then," called out Akimbo. "I hope you enjoyed that."

The two baboons stared at them. Their mouths were still full of the boys' lunch, so they did not say anything in reply.

Akimbo turned to Jen. "Did you notice something about the smaller one?" he asked.

Jen nodded. "Yes, I think I did. He was limping, wasn't he?"

"Yes," said Akimbo. "It was his left back paw. It was really swollen."

"Perhaps the leopard bit him," said Kosi. "Or slashed him with her claws."

"Maybe," said Jen. "But it hasn't made him any less brave, has it?"

TOMMY AND BEN

Over the next few days, the baboons settled down and began to range farther in search of food. Not all of them went off on these expeditions; the mothers and the very young baboons remained behind. Jen was happy to stay and watch them. She sat under her tree, looking through her telescope or binoculars, writing down what was happening among the rocks and trees where the troop lived.

"I'm just getting to know them now," she explained to the boys. "I'll come back and watch them later this year. I'll spend longer with them then."

Jen was now trying to figure out who was

who in the troop. As she identified the baboons, she gave them each a name. To the leader of the troop, a large male with a deep, rather angry bark she had given the name Hobo, but she let the boys choose names for some of the others. Akimbo selected the names for the two baboons who had stolen their sandwiches. He called them Tommy and Ben, after two boys in his class at school. Ben was the baboon with a limp.

"They're both a little bit greedy," he said, smiling. "Just like those two baboons."

Jen laughed at the joke. "All right," she said. "Tommy and Ben it is!"

If Tommy and Ben—the baboons—were greedy, then they were also very inquisitive. A couple of days after their first encounter with them, the two baboons started to take an interest in what was happening under the tree and decided to pay their watchers a visit. This time there was no food for them to steal, but that did not dampen their curiosity. Now they came even closer, so they were almost within reaching distance of the boys and Jen.

Akimbo took the opportunity to look at Ben's swollen foot. He had been right: it was almost twice the size of the baboon's other foot, and there was a dark area in the fur that looked as if blood had oozed out.

"It doesn't look too good," he whispered to Jen. "Look—it seems painful when he puts his weight on it."

"Anything could have happened," said Jen. "If we hadn't seen him limping a few days ago I would have thought that he might have been stung by a scorpion—baboons are always teasing scorpions and getting stung for it. But the swelling from a sting would have gone down by now."

Akimbo peered more closely at Ben, who looked back at him with open interest. That's when Akimbo saw it, and he tugged at Jen's sleeve to get her attention.

"Look," he said. "Look, there's a piece of wire!"

He had spotted the wire when Ben changed his position and stretched out his swollen leg. Now it was very visible, and there was no mistaking what it was.

"Ah!" said Jen. "So that's what it is. Poor thing—he must be in terrible pain. It's twisted around his leg there, you see, and cut into his flesh."

The thought of the pain Ben must be in made Akimbo wince. "We have to help him, Jen," he said. "We can't let him suffer."

Jen frowned. "I don't like the thought of him suffering either," she said. "But I'm not sure what we can do. We wouldn't be able to grab hold of him and take it off. He'd bite us badly if we tried that."

Kosi had an idea. "Couldn't we knock him out with one of those special darts the rangers use?" he asked. "Then, while he's asleep, we could deal with it."

"A good idea," said Jen. "But I'm afraid that I don't have one of those special darts. So . . ."

"But you do have a net," said Akimbo. "You have that mosquito net that you put over your sleeping bag at night."

Jen looked doubtful. "Do you think we could catch him with that? I'm not so sure."

"But we could," said Akimbo. "We know how greedy he is. If we brought some food down here, I'm sure he'd try to get it. And then we could throw the net over him . . ."

"And hold him down while Akimbo cuts the wire off his foot," interjected Kosi.

"Yes," said Akimbo. "That's what we could do. Please, Jen, let's give it a try."

It took a bit more persuading, but at last Jen agreed that they could try the boys' plan.

"I don't think it'll do my mosquito net much good," she said ruefully. "But I suppose it's more important to help poor Ben."

The next day, they went down to their place under the tree early and tied the net to one of the overhanging branches. When the piece of string holding up the net was released, it fell down like a billowing white cloud and covered whatever was beneath it. They tried it with Kosi, who pretended to be Ben for the trial. It worked perfectly, covering the boy with folds of material and making it impossible for him to move very much.

"But remember that Ben has much bigger teeth than Kosi," Jen warned. "And he won't be afraid to use them, either."

Akimbo knew that they would have to be very careful. Fortunately Jen had brought gloves with her just in case she had to handle a baboon, and she said that she would put those on and hold the back of Ben's head while Akimbo took hold of the wire. Kosi would try to grab Ben's front legs to keep him from scratching anybody.

"It will be three against one," said Akimbo.

"Or maybe three against two," warned Jen.

Akimbo wasn't sure what she meant.

Jen explained, "Baboons help one another," she said. "Tommy will see what's happening and will probably come to Ben's aid. So that makes two of them."

Akimbo had not thought of this. The possibility of another baboon attacking them while they tried to deal with Ben made the whole plan seem less likely to work!

"But don't worry," said Jen brightly. "I have an idea for what we can do about that. Just listen to this."

Akimbo and Kosi listened carefully as she explained what she had in mind. Then, rushing back to the hut, the two boys went to fetch the special things Jen needed for her plan. It was a very funny plan, Akimbo thought, but it just might work.

BABOON RESCUE

When they returned to their observation post under the tree the next morning they were carrying much more than usual. Akimbo had the mosquito net, which was bundled up tightly but was still heavy and unwieldy. Kosi was carrying a large bag of food, and Jen had a big can of sticky molasses and a long pole.

Akimbo's mother had given them the molasses when they left the ranger station so the boys could have it on their sandwiches. They both liked the sweet taste, and ever since they had arrived at the hut they had enjoyed it at every meal.

"Are you sure that baboons like molasses?"

Akimbo asked as they walked along the path to the hut. He was still a little bit doubtful as to whether Jen's plan would work, although she seemed confident enough.

"They love it," she said. "They can't resist it."

At first Akimbo said nothing. He wanted the plan to work, but it seemed that so much could go wrong with it. "Let's hope," he said.

They soon arrived at the tree. Akimbo dumped the net on the ground while Kosi, who was a good climber, scaled the trunk of the tree and edged slowly out along one of the overhanging branches. There he looped a piece of string around the branch so that both ends hung down to the ground. Then, while Akimbo tied one end of the string to the top of the net, Kosi climbed back down.

At first there was no sign of the baboons that morning.

"They're off looking for food," said Jen. "But don't worry—they'll come back. We'll just have to wait."

Jen was right. After a few hours—hours that

Akimbo thought dragged by very slowly—the baboons returned. They knew this was about to happen when they heard barking—those gruff barks that baboons exchange with one another. Then there were movements in the tall grass and dark shapes clambering up over rocks.

Something was exciting the baboons, and they began to chatter and grunt once they reached the rocks. Then there was an indignant squealing sound, and two smaller baboons broke away from the group and ran over to another rock, where they cowered, shrieking and baring their teeth at the others.

Jen watched this with interest. "They've been punished for something," she said to the boys. "They're younger males, those two. Two boys. And they've been told off by a more senior male."

"What did they do wrong?" asked Kosi.

Jen smiled. "They probably didn't treat him with proper respect," she said. "Baboons have ranks, you know. There are the powerful and important, and then those who are not. The powerful ones remind the others who's the boss from time to time!"

"It sounds unfair," said Akimbo. In fact, it sounded like bullying to him, but he knew that was the way wild animals were. There was always somebody who was senior, and the junior ones had to remember this.

Now it was time to put out the food. Jen said that the baboons would smell the food if they put it on the ground near the tree, and with any luck Tommy and Ben would come over to investigate, as they had the day before.

For an hour or so nothing happened, and Akimbo wondered whether the plan would work at all. Perhaps Tommy and Ben weren't hungry, he thought. If they had been out looking for food, maybe they had already found some and wouldn't be tempted by the smell of human food.

It was Kosi who gave the warning. "I think I see something," he whispered, tugging at Jen's sleeve. "Look over there."

What Kosi had seen was Tommy and Ben. The two baboons had detached themselves from the rest and made their way through the grass toward the observation post. Now they were just a short distance away, and there was no doubt that they were interested in the food.

"I hope that Ben comes first," whispered Akimbo. "Come on, Ben! Delicious food!"

It was as if the baboon had heard him. Tommy remained sitting on the ground—he seemed more nervous than Ben, even though he was the bigger of the two. Ben now moved forward, looking at the watching people from time to time, but clearly much more interested in the food lying on the ground directly beneath the branch of the large tree. And in the tree itself, suspended directly above the food, was the mosquito net.

Ben edged forward, gingerly, and Akimbo and the others held their breath in anticipation. Then, after a quick glance in the direction of the people, Ben reached forward to snatch the food.

That was Akimbo's signal to act. With a sharp tug on the string, he released the mosquito net. Down it fell—billowing like a large parachute—over the surprised baboon below.

There was a tremendous howl from Ben, but he was entirely caught in the folds of the net and was unable to run. Now Jen stepped forward and pulled the cloth tighter around him, binding him up in folds of white net. Ben screamed in fury, but his struggles only seemed to make the net tighter.

When the net fell upon Ben, Tommy had jumped backward in fright. But once his fear had been dispelled, he advanced toward the struggling bundle of cloth to see if he could help his friend. As he did so, he bared his fangs at the people to warn them off. It seemed as if he were saying, "This is my friend; you keep away!"

Jen gave a signal to Akimbo and the second part of the plan went into operation. At the end of the long pole was a sticky bundle of bread, secured by string. Akimbo pushed this toward Tommy, who turned and stared at it suspiciously.

"Come on, Tommy," muttered Akimbo. "Delicious, sticky syrup!"

Naturally the baboon understood none of this, but he did seem to realize that what he was being offered at the end of the pole was a treat that smelled more delicious than anything he had ever encountered before. Could he resist it?

No, he could not. It was just too much for any baboon, and he reached out and took the syrup-soaked lump of bread. Of course, this meant that his hands were soon covered with the sticky substance, and this puzzled him. Tommy started to lick at the syrup, found it delicious, and became completely absorbed in the task of getting the syrup off. Soon it was transferred from his hands to the fur on his face and below his jaws. It was all very confusing for him, even if it was also a very tasty thing.

With Tommy distracted in this way, Jen, with the help of the two boys, was able to extract Ben's leg from the folds of the net. As Jen touched the injured flesh, the baboon gave a muffled howl from within the net. It was painful for him, but they had to do it, and with the help of a pair of pliers they soon cut through the wire.

Jen held up the cruel twist of wire once she and Akimbo had finished unwinding it from Ben's leg. It was covered in blood and baboon hair. "No wonder he was in pain," she said. "Look at that. It cut right into him."

With their first aid complete, they were now able to untangle the net and let Ben go free. It was not easy—he struggled and squealed a great deal—but eventually they had the net off him. Once that happened, he shot off at speed, dragging his injured leg behind him, stopping occasionally to lick at his wound. Tommy ran off with him, also stopping from time to time—in his case, to lick not at a wound but at parts of his fur that were now completely covered in syrup.

OFF TRACK

They had only a few more days at the camp before they were due to go home. Nothing much happened in the baboon troop during this time, although one of the females gave birth one afternoon, and that created a lot of interest for the other baboons. It seemed as if the whole group wanted to welcome the new arrivals, and they crowded around to do so. Not everyone was allowed to get close to the babies, although one or two of the mothers' close friends were permitted to touch them. Jen noted all of this—she now knew just about all the members of the troop and knew, too, where they were in the pecking order.

On their last day at the observation post there was not very much for the two boys to do. Jen was watching the baboons, and when Akimbo asked if he and Kosi could go and explore on the other side of the valley, she saw no reason why they should not. There had been no sign of any lions in the area and it seemed safe enough, as long as they did not go too far. There was also very little chance of their being surprised by a leopard—if there had been any leopards nearby, the baboons would have let them know by their behavior.

The two boys set off, following the path of a dried-up riverbed. They saw monkeys in the trees at the edge of the river and a small family of warthogs trotting through the bush with their tails erect, like little flags. But apart from them, it seemed as if any other animals were taking their afternoon rest.

They had walked for some distance when Akimbo noticed fresh ostrich tracks.

"We could follow these tracks," he said to Kosi. "Have you ever seen an ostrich close up?"

Kosi had not and was excited by the idea. So together the two boys followed the tracks left by the large birds. Akimbo had been taught how to track by his father and was eager to put his skills to the test, and here, on the sandy soil of that part of the valley, it was not difficult to see the route that their quarry had taken.

Kosi was thrilled to be tracking with his cousin. He listened carefully as Akimbo explained how a set of footprints could tell you so much. Some of the clues were simple. For instance, if the soil disturbed by the animal's hoof or foot was still damp, that meant that the creature had passed by very recently. That was very straightforward, and even somebody who had never tracked before could think of that.

But some of the things that Akimbo described were much more surprising. Kosi would never have thought that you could tell the speed at which an animal had been traveling merely by looking at its tracks in the sand. Yet you could—and Akimbo explained how.

"You see these tracks here," he said to Kosi. "They're far apart, aren't they? That means the animal was running. It must have

been in a hurry. And if you see them like that and then they suddenly turn, it means they were being chased by something."

These fascinating lessons continued while the two boys walked past the end of the valley and onto a wide plain beyond. It was still possible to make out the ostrich tracks at the end of the valley, but when they reached the plain it became much more difficult.

"I think that they must have gone that way," said Akimbo, pointing in the direction of a clump of tall trees. Kosi nodded, but there was something in his cousin's voice that sounded uncertain. Did Akimbo really know which way the birds had gone, or was he just guessing?

They walked for another hour or so before Akimbo stopped and sat down on a rock.

"I'm sorry," he said. "I've lost them. The ground here is too grassy."

"It doesn't matter," said Kosi, glancing up at the sun, which was now high in the sky. "It's about time we made our way back to the camp."

Akimbo stood up, stretched, and looked around. "Yes," he said. "It's about time." And then he paused. When he looked around, he had expected to know exactly which direction they would have to follow to get back to the camp. Now he found, to his surprise, that it was far from clear which way they would have to go.

He looked at Kosi, who returned his stare, shrugging his shoulders. "I'm sorry," Kosi said. "I wasn't paying attention. I have no idea where we are." He paused. "Maybe we could follow our own tracks backward."

It was a good suggestion, but from the moment Akimbo looked down at the ground he knew that it would not be possible—it was one thing to follow tracks on sand, it was another to follow them on grass; in fact, it was impossible. And for the last half hour they had been on grass.

"Are we lost?" asked Kosi miserably.

Akimbo shook his head. "I'm sure that we came that way," he said, pointing in the direction of a small granite hillock.

It did not seem familiar to Kosi, but he

had no alternative but to trust his cousin's instincts and follow him.

They walked for hours. Once they arrived at the hillock they realized that it was not the right place, and so they began to retrace their steps. Then Akimbo changed his mind and they went off in another direction.

Kosi was worried. He had felt safe with his cousin, but it was hard to feel confident when Akimbo kept changing his mind. And now, judging by the position of the sun and the length of the shadows, it was well past four o'clock in the afternoon. At six o'clock the skies would begin to darken and night would fall. If they could not find their way by then, they would be out in the bush at a time when wild animals would be on the prowl. Leopards. Lions. What chance would two small boys have against creatures like that?

Akimbo himself was very worried. He imagined what Jen must be thinking, and he wondered what she would do. Would she try to find them, or would she make her way back by herself to the ranger camp and get his father to come to the rescue? Whatever happened, he would have to explain just how he had lost the way, and he was sure that his father would think twice about letting him go out again by himself. And that would be very hard to take.

Help!

When night falls in Africa, it falls with suddenness. One moment the sky is blue and empty; the next it has faded and stars begin to appear. Then, as the last traces of light go from the sky, there is nothing but darkness covering the land like a velvet cloth.

"We'll have to find somewhere safe to spend the night," said Akimbo.

"If there *is* anywhere safe," said Kosi. Looking around him, he could not see anywhere that looked like a good place to stay for the night. There were no caves in the rocks, no trees with low branches on which they could lie, as if in a hammock.

Akimbo was also looking, and he, too, could see nothing. Yet they could hardly stay out there, unprotected from the dangers of the night.

"Maybe we could try shouting," said Kosi. The suggestion did not sound very convincing, even to him, but he thought it was better than nothing. "There may be some huts near here," he added lamely. "Or a ranger tent . . ."

Akimbo did not think that there was much point in shouting for help, but at least it amounted to doing something. So he looked out into the darkness, took a deep breath, and shouted *Help!* at the top of his voice. Kosi did the same, and then the two of them stopped to listen. It would have been wonderful if an answering voice had come back, but there was nothing; just the faint echo of *help* bouncing off the hard rocks and then disappearing into the night air.

They repeated their cries again and again, each time with no result. And then, just when they were about to give up, they heard something.

"What was that?" asked Akimbo. He felt

anxious. What if by shouting out they were merely giving away their position to some predator—perhaps to a lion?

The sound came again, and it was not the roar of a lion or the cough of a leopard: it was a barking sound.

Akimbo and Kosi stood stock still. A baboon! Then Akimbo shouted out again and, after a short delay, there again came an answering bark.

Akimbo had noted the direction from which the bark had come. "It was over there," he whispered to Kosi. "And it's not far away."

Carefully the two boys made their way through the darkness, trying to avoid the thorn bushes and the other obstacles that lay in their way. They half-walked, half-ran, so eager were they to find the baboon. If this was one of the baboons from the troop, then all they would have to do was follow it through the darkness until they reached its sleeping place. Once they found that, it would be simple to locate the observation post and their camp.

Suddenly Akimbo stopped. From a clump of bushes had come a grunt.

"What is it?" whispered Kosi, his heart hammering with fear. He knew that leopards grunted, and if they had stumbled upon a leopard . . .

It was not a leopard. As the two boys stood there in fright, a dark shape emerged from the bushes—a baboon. And even in the darkness, the boys could make out something special about this baboon: it was limping.

"Ben!" whispered Akimbo, his heart giving a leap of joy. It was like finding a friend again when you thought that all was lost.

The baboon stopped and seemed to stare at the boys for a while, as if sizing them up. Then he gave another grunt and began to amble off into the shadows with that curious loping way that baboons have. Without saying anything to each other, Akimbo and Kosi began to follow him, keeping a respectful distance so as not to frighten him, but close enough to make sure that they did not lose sight of their rescuer.

They were much closer to the camp than they had thought, and it was only thirty minutes or so later that they saw, in the darkness

ahead of them, the pinprick of light that they recognized as the camp.

"Thank you, Ben!" Akimbo called out, and then, closely followed by Kosi, he began to run toward the light.

Jen hugged both boys so tightly that they could hardly breathe.

"I was worried sick," she said. "I waited until the sun went down, and then I got ready to drive back to the ranger camp. But then I asked myself what would happen if you turned up and discovered the camp empty. So I decided to wait until morning. Thank goodness I did."

She fed the boys a delicious hot soup while they told her the story of their adventure.

"It was all my fault," said Akimbo. "I was trying to track ostriches and—"

Jen did not let him finish. "Let's not worry about whose fault it was," she said. "The important thing is that you're back safely. That's all that counts."

Akimbo was relieved that he was not being scolded for what happened, but he felt, too, that he had learned a lesson about being out in the bush: never forget where you are; always take note of and remember the things you've walked past. In this way you will be able to use landmarks to make your way home. It was not a lesson that he would forget in a hurry.

They also told Jen about how Ben had saved them, and she listened very carefully to that.

"I'm not sure if he would have done that deliberately," she said. "Perhaps he just happened to be there. And then he happened to be coming home."

Akimbo was silent. He knew that he should not make up feelings and thoughts for animals—the things they did usually had reasons that were entirely their own and had nothing to do with people. But he was sure, in his heart of hearts, that Ben was repaying them for getting the wire off his leg—he was sure of that. And just by looking at his cousin, Akimbo knew that Kosi thought the same way.

The next day they packed up the camp

and prepared to leave the area. As they made their way back to the waiting truck, Akimbo saw a small group of baboons watching them from the low branch of a tree. At that distance, he could not make out the features of any of the baboons, but he was sure that one of them was Ben.

"Good-bye," he said under his breath. "And thank you."

The baboons watched. One of them raised a hand. Was he waving farewell, or was he just brushing away a fly?

Akimbo decided that he was waving.

DID YOU KNOW?

• There are five types of baboon: the olive baboon, the chacma, the hamadryas, the Guinea (all found in different parts of Africa), and the yellow baboon, found in Africa but also in some countries in the Middle East.

• Baboons are known to be dog faced and have muzzles. They are from the primate order but are different from monkeys in that they don't have tails.

• Baboons live on the ground and are omnivorous, which means they eat everything— from grass to small antelopes! They have been known to raid human villages for food. They also have a bit of a sweet tooth and like foraging sweet gum from the bark of fever trees.

- Normally waking between seven and eight in the morning, baboons will descend from the trees and groom one another while the younger ones play.

- In ancient Egypt the baboon was an important religious symbol—strange, considering baboons are not native to Egypt.

- Scientists have discovered that, despite not being part of the same genetic family as human beings, baboons are in fact very similar to us in the way that they socially interact, with their group sustained by a strict hierarchy and rules.

- A pack of baboons is called a "troop."

- In the wild, the average lifespan of a baboon is thirty years, but in captivity they can live much longer.

- As a means of protecting themselves from predators—the most threatening of which are human beings—baboons will sleep in high trees and cliffs. They are also often hunted by leopards, lions, cheetahs, and wild dogs, although their size can make them formidable opponents!

• Baboons can travel up to ten miles a day moving in an organized unit, fanning out to feed and forage for food to bring back to their base.

• Baboons have dozens of ways of communicating to one another using their voices, and like us they use gestures as well –including yawning to show their teeth as an act of aggression.

• Baboons also mourn the loss of their friends and family. According to one report, when a baboon was killed on a road in eastern Uganda, the troop surrounded the female's body and refused to move for half an hour! Another report described seeing baboons throwing sticks and stones at passing cars after the death of one of their young on a road.

• Despite their sympathetic reactions to traumatic events, baboons can still get pretty nasty! Male baboons don't take kindly to intruders and will often fight each other for dominance over the females.

• Baboons exist as a large population because, like us, they are extremely adaptable and can weather most conditions—and are obviously not shy of stealing an odd goat or two from their human neighbors. They mostly prefer savannahs and dry places, but some do live in rainforests.

A Note on the Author

ALEXANDER MCCALL SMITH has written more than fifty books, including the *New York Times* bestselling No. 1 Ladies' Detective Agency mysteries and The Sunday Philosophy Club series. A professor of medical law at Edinburgh University, he was born in what is now Zimbabwe and taught law at the University of Botswana. He lives in Edinburgh, Scotland.

Visit him at WWW.ALEXANDERMCCALLSMITH.COM.

A Note on the Illustrator

LEUYEN PHAM is the illustrator of numerous award-winning books for children including *Big Sister, Little Sister* (which she also wrote); *Sing-Along Song*; *Piggies in a Polka*; and *Freckleface Strawberry*. She lives in San Francisco, California.

Visit her at WWW.LEUYENPHAM.COM.

AFRICAN WILDLIFE FOUNDATION®

You can learn all about elephants and lions and cheetahs and zebras and giraffes and other wildlife by visiting the African Wildlife Foundation at www.awf.org.

After you learn about the wild animals, you can help save them—by supporting the African Wildlife Foundation.

The African Wildlife Foundation has worked with the people of Africa for forty-five years. They train park rangers, like Akimbo's father, to protect wildlife and catch poachers. They give scholarships to girls and boys like Akimbo so they can grow up and learn to be scientists who protect Africa's mighty rivers and great forests.